POKéMON ADVENTURES™

Issue 2
Wanted: Pikachu

Story by **Hidenori Kusaka**
Art by **Mato**

English Adaptation by
Gerard Jones

Based on the game by:
Tsunekazu Ishihara & **Satoshi Tajiri**

POKéMON ADVENTURES
Issue 2:
Wanted: Pikachu

Story/Hidenori Kusaka
Art/Mato

English Adaptation/Gerard Jones

Translation/Kaori Inoue
Touch-up & Lettering/Dan Nakrosis
Graphics & Design/Carolina Ugalde
Editing/William Flanagan

Editor-in-Chief/Hyoe Narita
Publisher/Seiji Horibuchi

First published by
Shogakukan, Inc. in Japan.

First printing,October 1999
2nd printing, November 1999

Published by Viz Comics
P.O. Box 77064
San Francisco, CA 94107

For advertising opportunities, call:
Oliver Chin
Director of Sales and Marketing
(415) 546-7073 ext. 128

CONTENTS

WANTED PIKACHU! ④

GET IT!

HURRY!

RUMBLE! RUMBLE!

PEWTER CITY, IN THE WEST

THERE IT GOES!

RUMBLE! RUMBLE!

WET!

PDMDM

HUH?

FLUTTER!

PWAP!

WANTED

PIKACHU

Mischievous electric mouse. Reward for capture. ♪

·Pewter City Merchants Association

SO THAT'S WHAT ALL THE FUSS IS ABOUT.

GUESS I'LL GIVE 'EM A HAND!

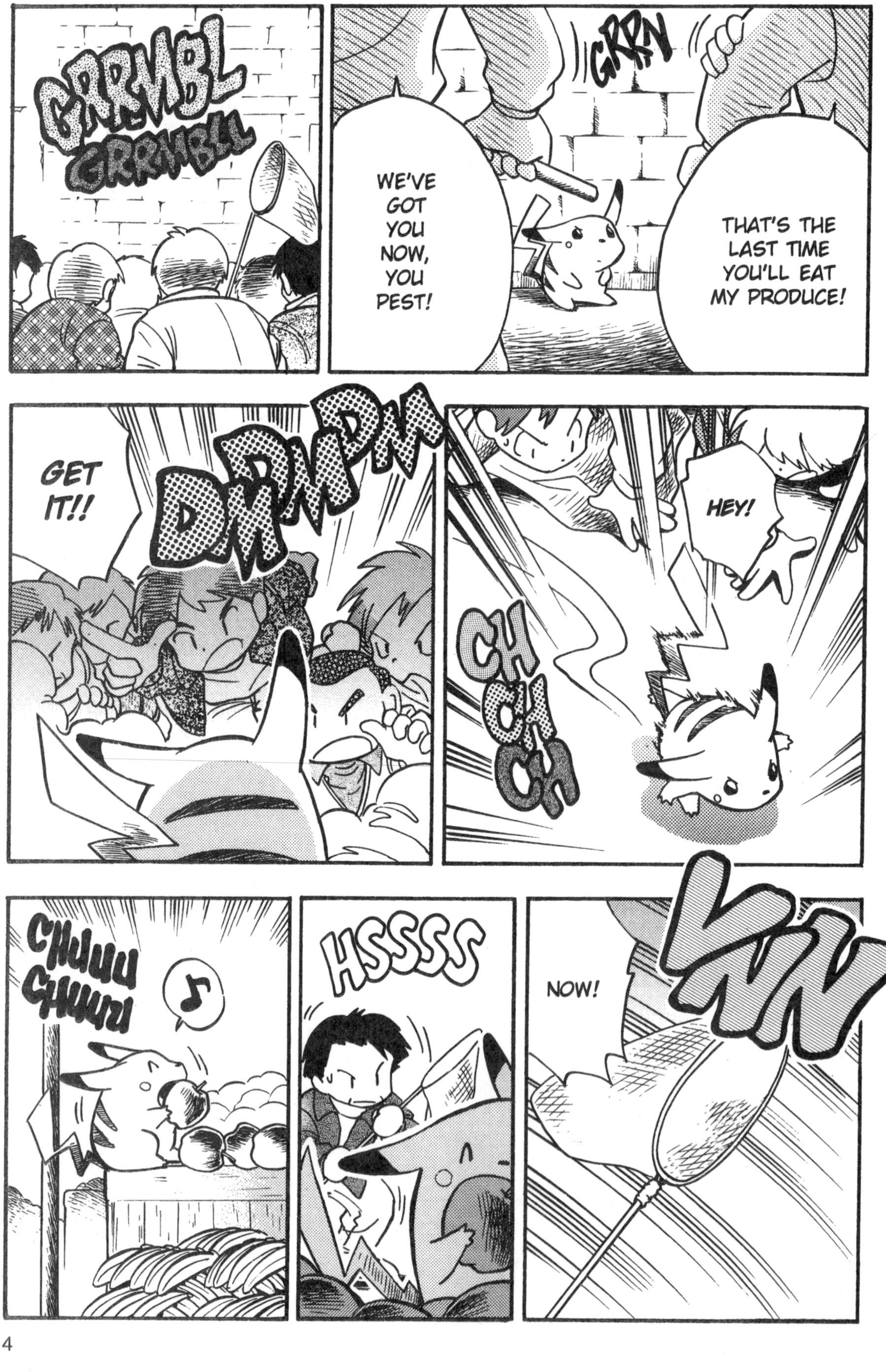
GRRMBL
GRRMBLL
GRRN
WE'VE GOT YOU NOW, YOU PEST!
THAT'S THE LAST TIME YOU'LL EAT MY PRODUCE!
GET IT!!
DMDMDM
HEY!
CH CH CH CH
CHUUU CHUUU
♪
HSSSS
NOW!
VUN

HEY, IT'S GETTING AWAY AGAIN!

UHHHH

GET IT!!

DM!DM!DM!

TSK. I CAN'T WATCH ANY MORE OF THIS.

O-- KAY ...

POM

BULBA-SAUR--
GO!

PO-NNN BOM!

mrgl mrgl

PI!?

mrgl mrgl mrgl

OOOO!

A POKÉ-MON!

mrmr mrmr

GRRN

Sneer

CHAK!

AUUGH!

OH... MAN...

IT'S NO USE...

mrg! mrg!

P!⁉

NOW IT'S *OUR* TURN.

BULBA-SAUR, ATTACK!

BLB!

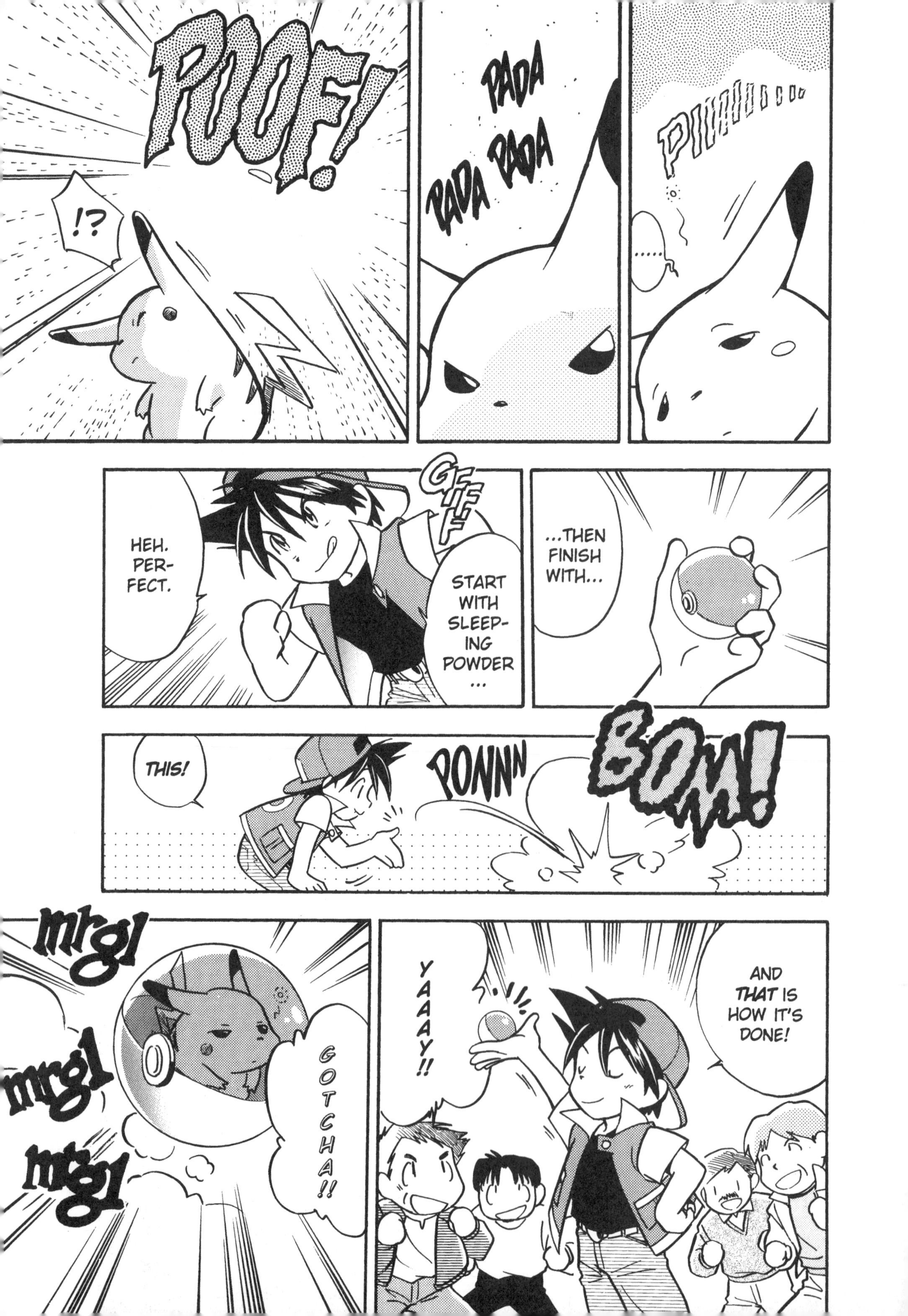

POOF!
!?
PADA PADA PADA
PIIIIiiii
......
HEH. PER-FECT.
GFF
START WITH SLEEP-ING POWDER ...
...THEN FINISH WITH...
THIS!
PONNN
BOM!
mrgl
mrgl
mrgl
GOTCHA!!
YAAAAY!!
AND THAT IS HOW IT'S DONE!

YOUNG MAN, YOU'VE SAVED US!

THAT PEST WAS RUINING OUR BUSINESSES!

WE WISH YOU'D COME A LONG TIME AGO!

WHERE ARE YOU FROM?

I'M FROM PALLET TOWN.

BUT WHAT BROUGHT YOU *HERE*?

GLMP GLMP

WANNA KNOW?

THEN JUST WATCH WHILE I...

DO THIS!

PIK PIK

PIPI!

PIKACHU

DATA

No. 025

Description
MOUSE
Categories
Type 1/ Electric
Height 1' 04"
Weight 13.0 lb
Attacks
Thundershock
Thunder Wave
Quick Attack

When several of these Pokémon gather, their electricity could build and cause lightning storms. Forest dwellers, they are few in number and are exceptionally rare. The pouches on their cheeks discharge electricity at their opponents. The Pikachu are believed to be highly intelligent.

HMMM...

SO THIS WILD PIKACHU CAME FROM THE VIRIDIAN FOREST TO SETTLE IN THIS CITY...

WHAT AN AWESOME DEVICE!

NOT YET.

THERE ARE MORE THAN A HUNDRED KINDS OF POKÉMON IN THE WORLD.

MY GOAL IS TO GET ALL THEIR DATA...AND CREATE THE COMPLETE POKÉDEX!

HUH?

GLMP
GLMP

HEY. COOL IT.

CHAKA CHAKA

WHAT'S WITH THIS THING?

WELP... OKAY THEN...

WHOA!!

PIXX

PIXX
PIXX

C'MON. DON'T BE SO STUBBORN.

HOW 'BOUT WE TRY TO BE FRIENDS?

CHUU

OKAY, PIKACHU?

......

AAAAGH!!

CHAKK

GEEZ. YOU MAY *LOOK* CUTE, BUT...

YOU'RE TAKING IT EASY, AREN'T YOU, RED?

SFIF

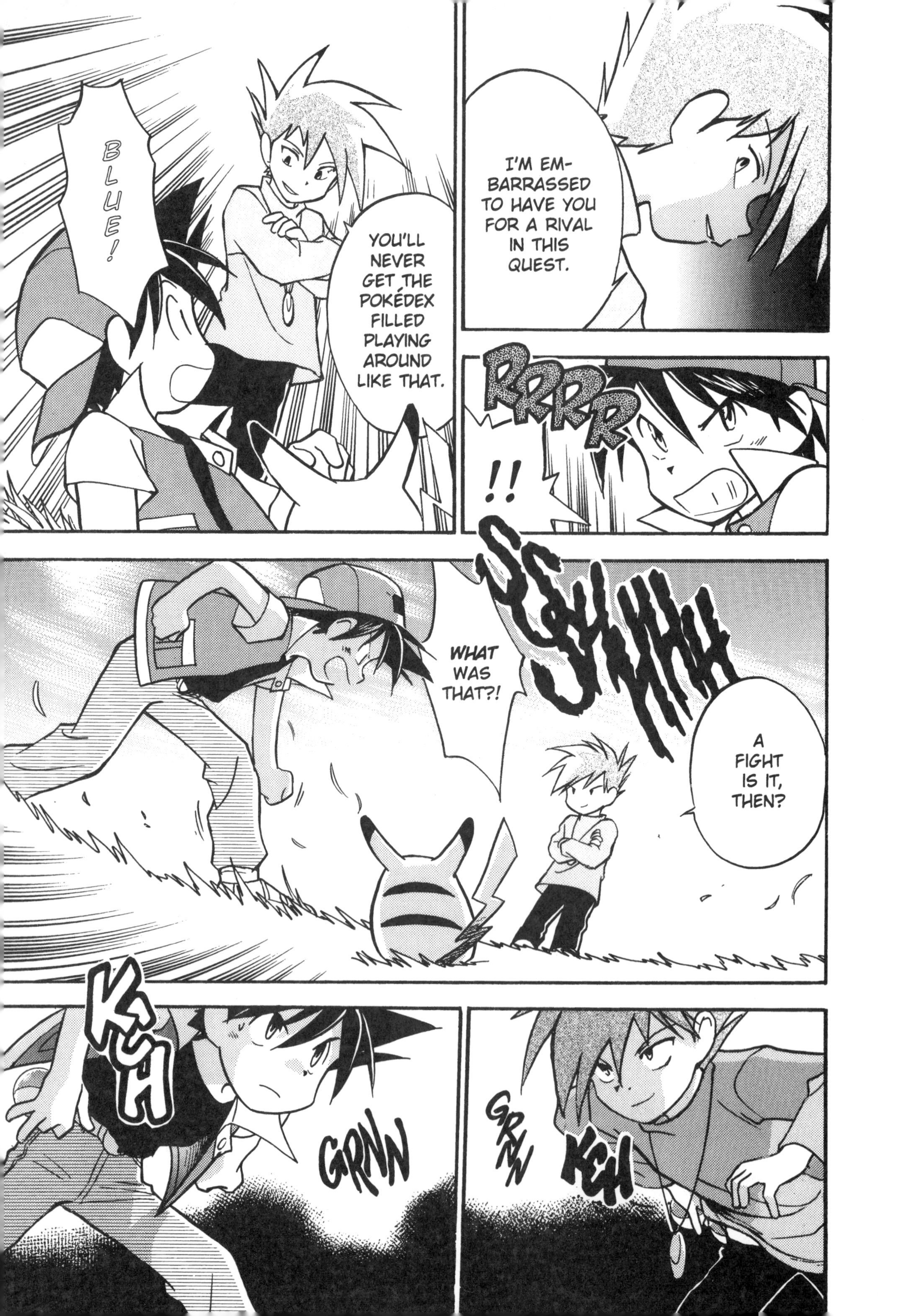
BLUE!
YOU'LL NEVER GET THE POKÉDEX FILLED PLAYING AROUND LIKE THAT.
I'M EM-BARRASSED TO HAVE YOU FOR A RIVAL IN THIS QUEST.
RRRR
!!
WHAT WAS THAT?!
A FIGHT IS IT, THEN?
KUH
GRNN
GRNN
KEH

BUT FIRST, MY IM-PETUOUS FRIEND...

ALLOW ME TO LET YOU IN ON SOME-THING.

?

THIS TOWN'S GYM LEADER, *BROCK*, IS LOOKING FOR SOMEONE COMPETENT TO FIGHT HIM.

I INTEND TO DO SO...AND WIN THE BOULDER BADGE.

THE BOULDER BADGE?

??

DON'T YOU KNOW?

THE BOULDER BADGE CAN BOOST THE ATTACK POWER OF YOUR POKÉMON.

EVERY POKÉ-MON TRAINER KNOWS THAT.

WELL, *SORRY* ...

YOU #!$@%!!

??

SO, THIS IS MY CHAL-LENGE...

LET'S SEE WHICH OF US CAN WIN THE BOULDER BADGE FIRST.

OF COURSE, IT SHOULDN'T BE MUCH OF A MATCH, IF YOU CAN'T EVEN TRAIN AN ELECTRIC MOUSE.

I'LL TAKE THAT CHALLENGE!

AND YOU'LL REGRET IT!

HA HA HA.

OH, AND ONE MORE THING.

BROCK IS A *ROCK* POKÉMON TRAINER.

YOUR LITTLE ELECTRIC MOUSE THERE WON'T DO ANY GOOD AGAINST HIM.

WELL, GOOD LUCK.

SHFFF

....

WHAT A JERK...

CALLING ALL FIGHTERS!!

PEWTER CITY GYM LEADER BROCK WILL TAKE ON ALL CHALLENGERS!

DATES AND TIMES:

CHALLENGER REQUIREMENTS:

PEWTER CITY:

SO THE NEXT CHALLENGE IS... TOMORROW AT NOON.

LET'S DO IT!

BLUE'LL BE SORRY HE EVER--

FIRST THING IN THE MORNING I NEED TO GO TO A POKÉMON CENTER...AND GET THESE GUYS HEALED!

WHOOPS. ALMOST FOR-GOT...

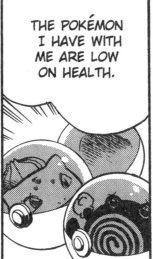

THE POKÉMON I HAVE WITH ME ARE LOW ON HEALTH.

NEXT DAY AT THE POKÉMON CENTER...

GRMBL GRMBL POKÉ CENTER

NOTICE

OUR CENTER WAS DAMAGED YESTERDAY BY UNKNOWN VANDALS. WE WILL REOPEN WHEN OUR MACHINES ARE RUNNING AGAIN. WE APOLOGIZE FOR ANY INCONVENIENCE THIS HAS CAUSED.

NO WAY...

RRRGHHH

KALANG! KRASH

THIS MEANS...

THE ONLY ONE WITH FULL POWER IS *THIS* ONE...

PAKA CHAKA

CHAPTER 5

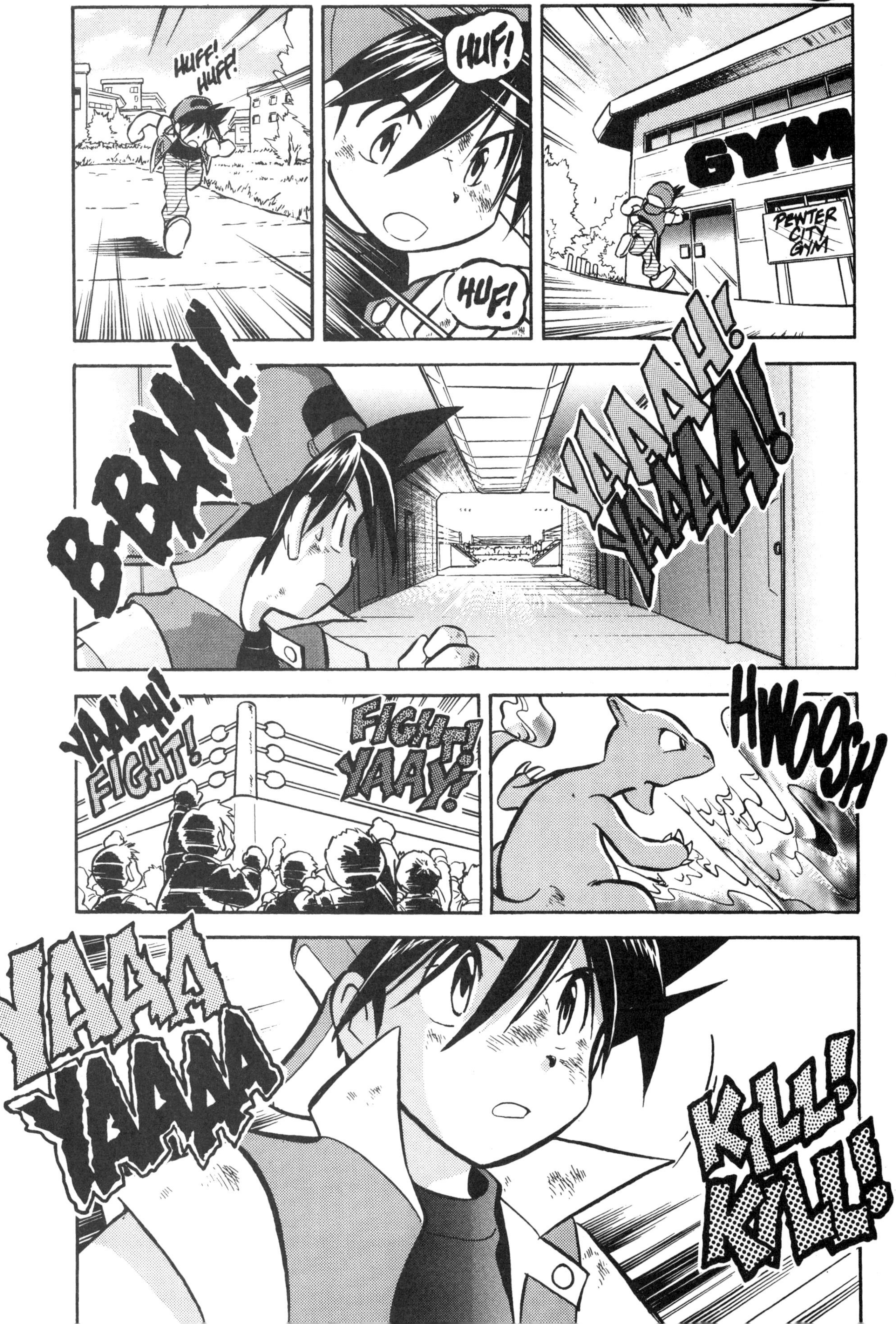

HUFF! HUFF!
HUF!
HUF!
GYM
PEWTER CITY GYM
B-BAM!
YAAAH! YAAAA!
YAAAH! FIGHT!
FIGHT! YAAY!
HWOOSH
YAAA YAAAA
KILL! KILL!

ONIX IS ON!

BLUE!!

FIGHT!

YAY!!

FWIP

B-BLOCK PRELIMINARY ROUND WILL START.

OOPS.

MY NAME'S RED. NUMBER 18.

Reception Desk

I'VE SEEN MY SHARE O' FIGHTS HERE, BUT HARDLY SEEN ANYBODY BLOW THROUGH THE PRELIMS TO GET TO BROCK.

FIGURES, WITH TH' PEWTER CITY GYM'S FINEST STANDIN' IN THE WAY.

COME ON, PUNK! LET'S GET THIS THING GOIN'!!

OKAY! YOU'RE ON!!

PUNI

OH, GREAT...

IT'S HOPE-LESS.

HE'S THE ONLY ONE AT FULL HEALTH...

BUT I COULDN'T TRAIN HIM!!

WELL, NOTHIN' ELSE TO DO NOW.

THEY'RE LOW ON HEALTH, BUT I'VE GOTTA FIGHT WITH THESE TWO.

IT DON'T LOOK LIKE MUCH TO ME!

DOES IT GOT ANY HEALTH LEFT, PUNK?

.....

KLAAAANG!

LET'S WIN IT WITH THE FIRST ATTACK, POLIWHIRL!!

PLOB! PLOB! PLOB!

!!

NOW-- "ICE BEAM"!!

VVIRRRRRR

KA-KLING!

AUGH!

PONN

WE CAN'T AFFORD TO TAKE EVEN ONE HIT-- OR WE'RE FINISHED!!

HUF HUF

THAT KID SHOWED ME SOMETHIN'!

HE'S FINISHIN' EVERY FIGHT WITH HIS FIRST ATTACK.

HE'S ONLY GOT TWO O' THE THINGS, BUT WITH THE SWIFT WATER POKÉMON...

WIGHAH...

AND THE POWER-FIGHTIN' GRASS POKÉMON, HE'S GOT GREAT BALANCE!

HE DOESN'T WASTE HIS ATTACKS EITHER. THE PUNK'S GOT STRATEGY!

KRAK!

HE DID IT AGAIN!!

YAAAAAY

NOW HE FINALLY GETS GYM LEADER BROCK!!

AT LAST! AN OPPONENT WORTHY OF ME!

AT THE GYM'S BACK ENTERANCE.

OH, C'MON, PIKACHU.

POLIWHIRL AND BULBASAUR ARE POOPED.

IF YOU'LL JUST DO IT THIS TIME... PLEASE!!

OKAY?

PWi!

WELL... WE'RE UP.

ZHZH ZH

KLAAANG!

NKH

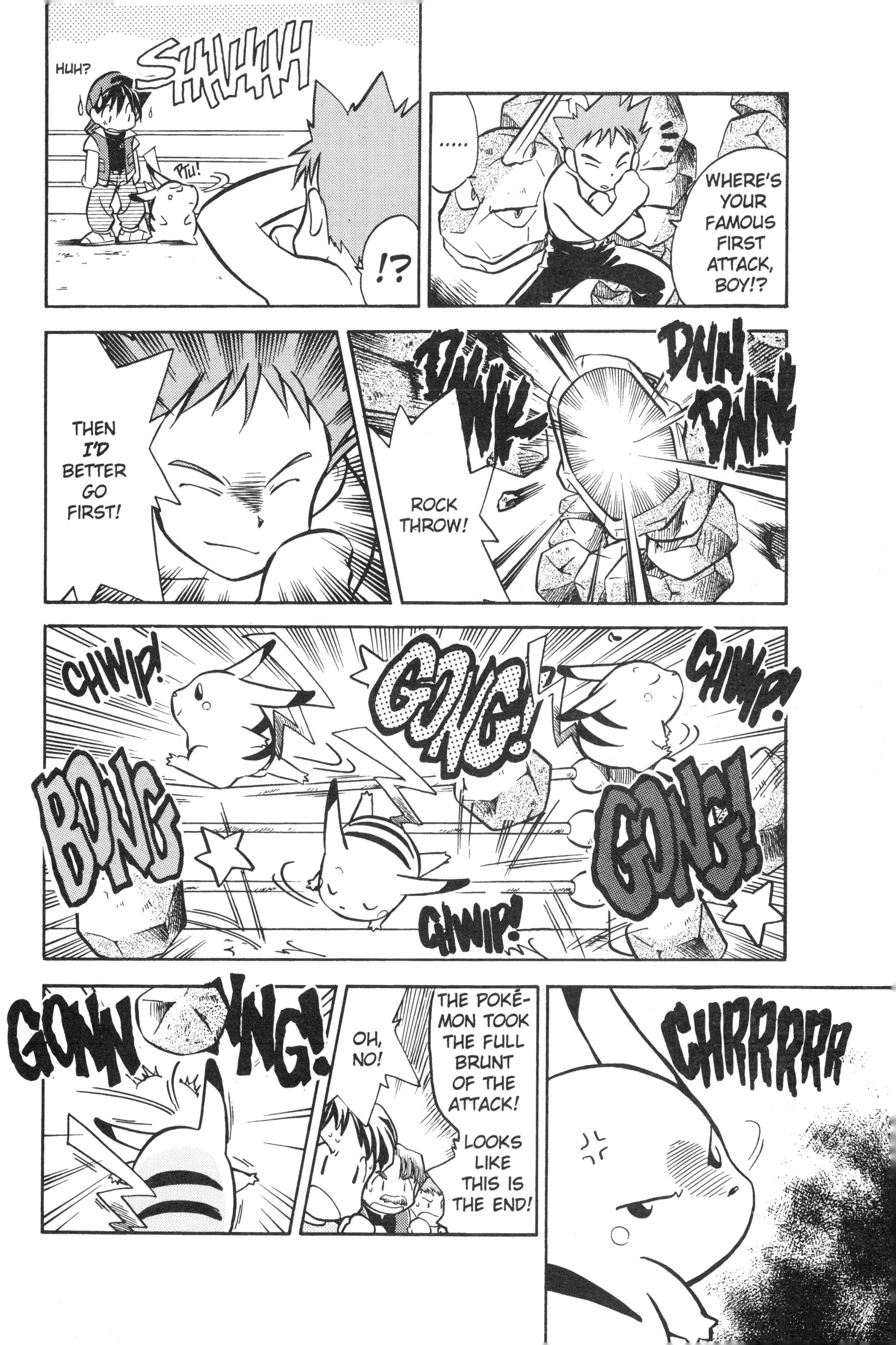
HUH?
SHWWH
PTU!
!?
.....
WHERE'S YOUR FAMOUS FIRST ATTACK, BOY!?
THEN I'D BETTER GO FIRST!
ROCK THROW!
DWNK
DNN DNN
CHWIP!
GONG!
CHWIP!
BONG
GONG!
CHWIP!
GONN NG!
OH, NO!
THE POKÉ-MON TOOK THE FULL BRUNT OF THE ATTACK!
LOOKS LIKE THIS IS THE END!
CHRRRRR

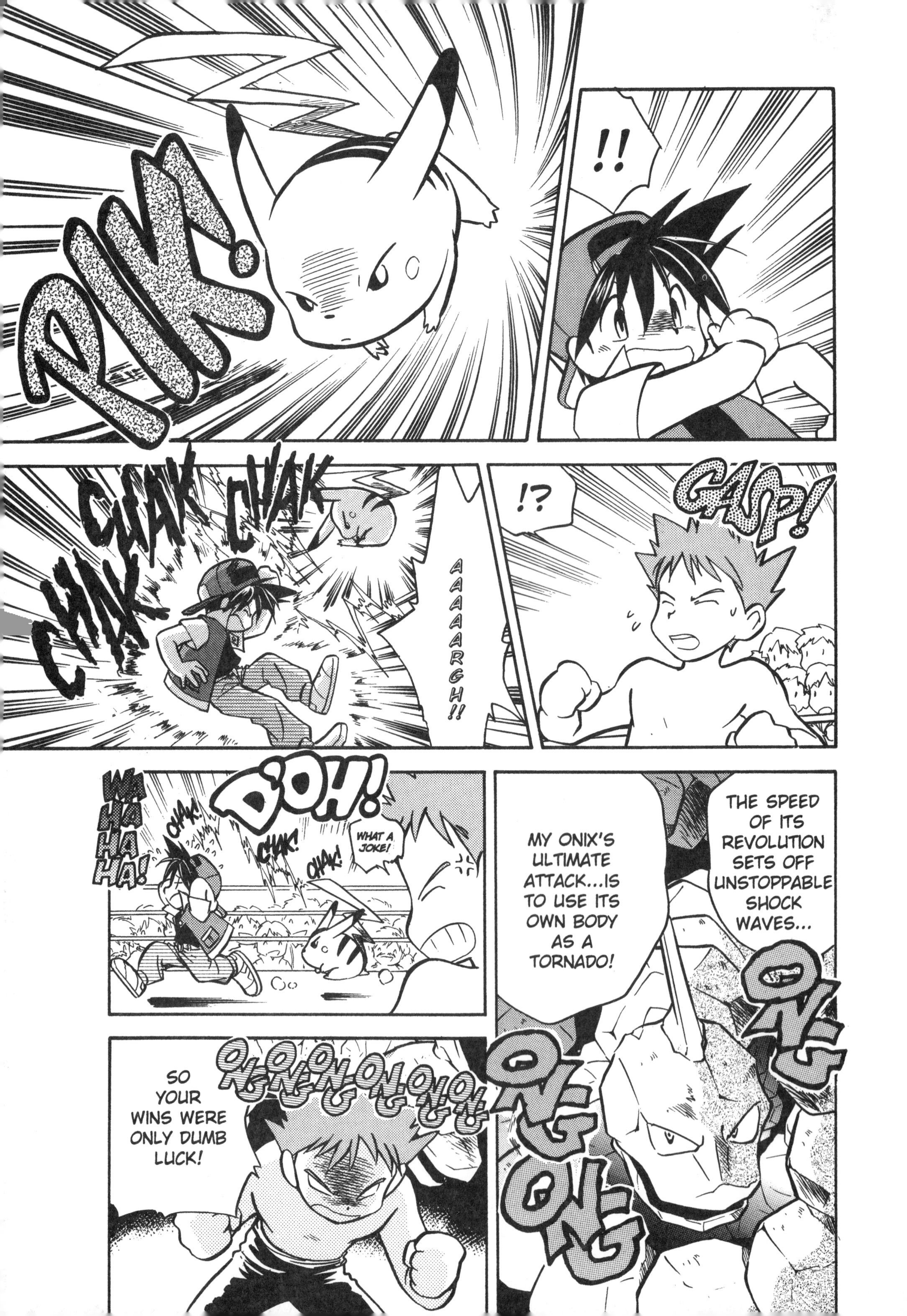
PIK!
!!
CHAK CHAK CHAK
AAAAAAARGH!!
!?
GASP!
WA HA HA HA HA!
D'OH!
CHAK!
CHAK!
CHAK!
WHAT A JOKE!
THE SPEED OF ITS REVOLUTION SETS OFF UNSTOPPABLE SHOCK WAVES...
MY ONIX'S ULTIMATE ATTACK...IS TO USE ITS OWN BODY AS A TORNADO!
ONG ONG ONG
SO YOUR WINS WERE ONLY DUMB LUCK!
ONGONGONGONGONGONGONG

UHHH...

GAGAGA KKKKK

GRONG!

GRONNNG!

IT'S A BIG ONE! WATCH OUT, PIKACHU!

THE FINAL STRIKE...

"SKULL BASH"!!

GROOOOOOO

GOONG!

GROSS

SHHHHHH

YOU OKAY?

pi!?

LOOK, YOU REALLY DON'T HAVE ANY OBLIGATION TO FIGHT FOR ME.

≥WHEW≤ ...I'M GLAD OF THAT...

I'M SORRY I FORCED YOU INTO THIS.

HOW 'BOUT WE TRY TO BE FRIENDS?

FEH. WE WON'T MISS THIS TIME!

RRRRR

ONIX- ATTACK!!

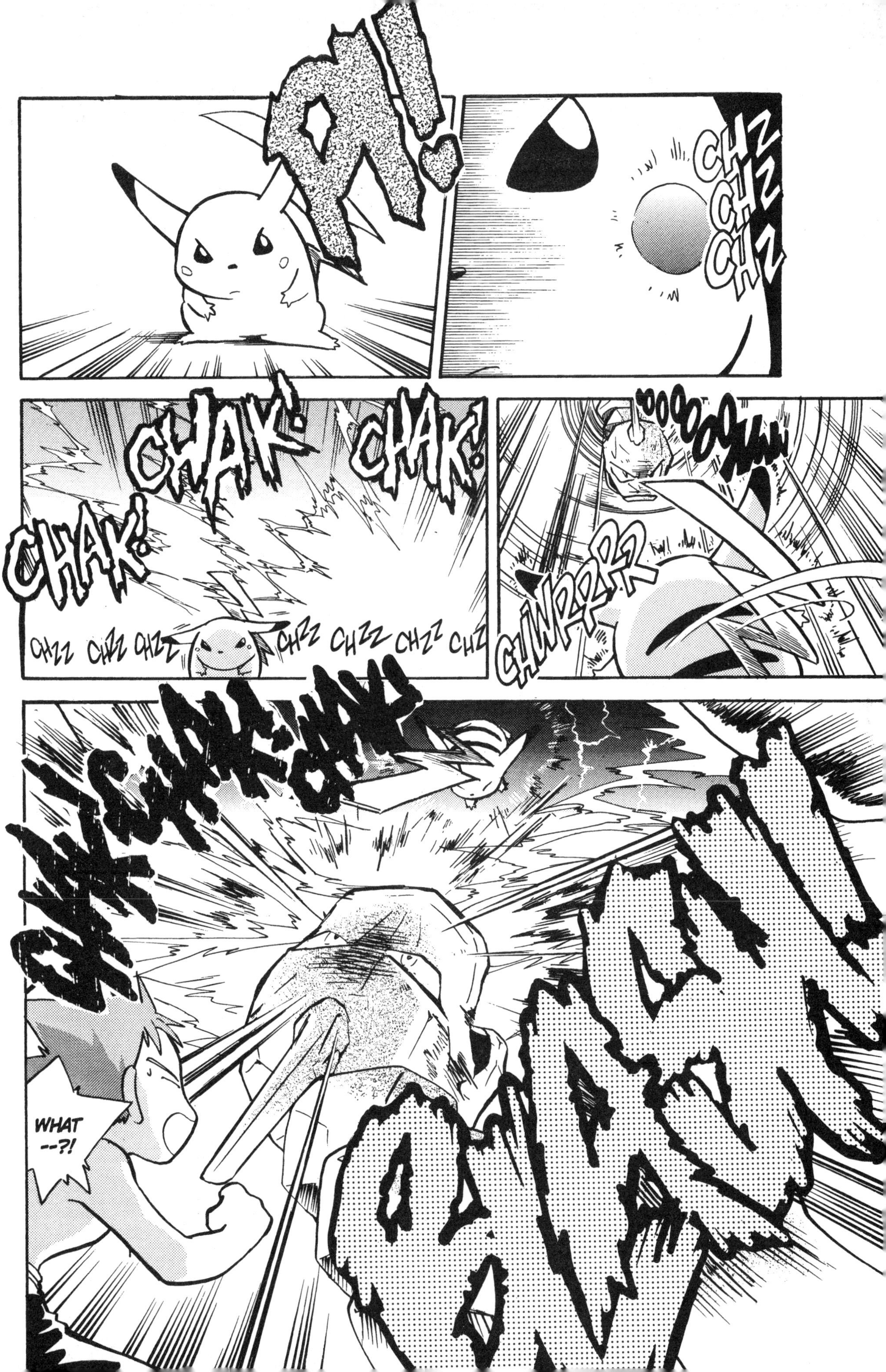
?!
CHZ CHZ CHZ
CHAK! CHAK! CHAK!
CHZZ CHZZ CHZZ CHZZ CHZZ CHZZ CHZ
CHWRRRR
WHAT --?!

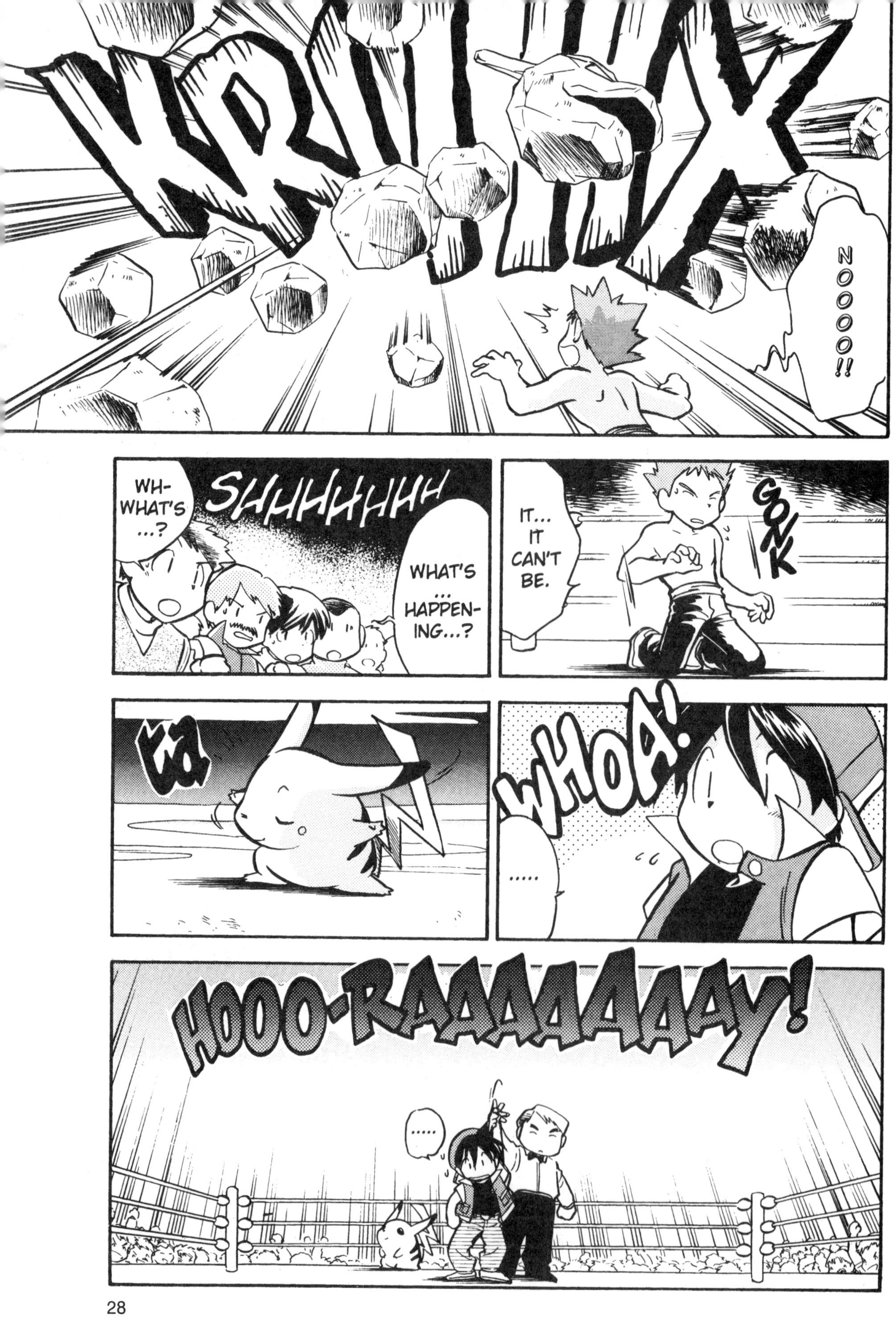
KRUUMX
NOOOOO!!
WH-WHAT'S ...?
SHHHHHHHH
WHAT'S ... HAPPEN-ING...?
IT... IT CAN'T BE.
GONK
WHOA!
.....
HOOO-RAAAAAAAY!
.....

SO BLUE AND I ENDED UP BEING THE ONLY ONES TO WIN THE BOULDER BADGE.

THANKS, PIKACHU.

I COULDN'T HAVE DONE IT WITHOUT YOU.

.....

THESE ARE POLIWHIRL AND BULBA-SAUR.

THEY'RE GOOD FRIENDS OF MINE.

WE'D LOVE TO HAVE YOU WITH US... IF YOU'LL HAVE US!

SHAKE ON IT ...?

chuuuu

? PIK!

EE-AAAARGH!!

CHAK! CHAK! CHAK!

WHAT'S THE IDEA?!

CHZ CHZ CHZ

JUST WHEN I THOUGHT I WAS FINALLY GETTING SOMEWHERE ...!!

hff hff

Drrp

GRRN

GYAOOOOO

gasp!

IT'S THE HYDRO PUMP! STARYU, GET AWAY!!

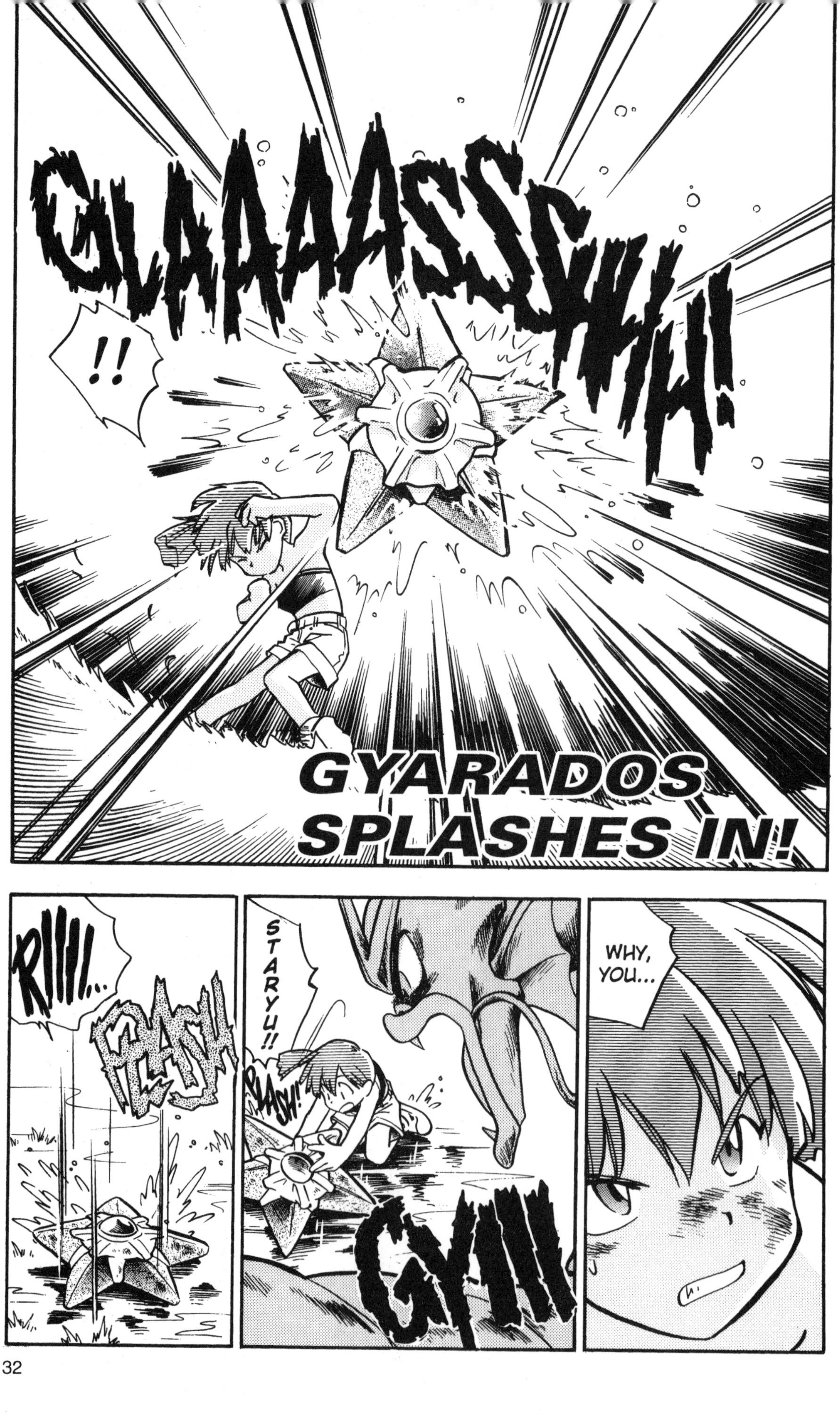
GLAAASSHH!
!!
GYARADOS SPLASHES IN!
RIIII...
PLASH
STARYU!!
PLASH!
GYIII
WHY, YOU...

TAKING ON A PRETTY BIG ONE, AREN'T YOU?

!

LET ME HELP.

STAY BACK, YOU! THIS IS DANGEROUS!

HEH HEH.

I'LL BE FINE! I'M NOT JUST *ANY* KID!

AND BY THE WAY--THE NAME'S NOT "YOU"!

SPECIFICALLY ...IT'S RED!

OKAY, BULBASAUR ...GO!

BBW!

A POKÉMON!

YOU'RE A POKÉMON TRAINER, TOO?

......

WATCH IT! IT'S THE HYDRO PUMP!

HUH...?

IZZAT POKÉMON SMILING...?

HEH...NO WATER ATTACK'S GONNA WORK A GRASS POKÉMON!

BLP!

BSH!

NOW IT'S OUR TURN!

BULBASAUR ...ATTACK!!

SRRRRRR...

GNGNG

GYAAAR!?

THE LEECH SEED?

YOU GOT IT!

NOW'S OUR CHANCE! RECOVER!

OKAY, STARYU-- YOUR WOUNDS ARE HEALED!

HEY... NOW *THAT* IS A SWEET TRICK!

SHALL WE TRY DOUBLE DATING?

WE SHALL!

BULBASAUR!!

STARYU!!

VINE WHIP!

SIIIH

BUBBLE-BEAM!

RRUP

RRUPRRUP

GYAAAAA

LAST BUT NOT LEAST.. THE POKÉ BALL!

POOOM

BOM

rrrgl mrrgl mrrgl

mrrgl mrrgl

SHHHHAAA

GOT HIM!

.....

PHEW!!

TH-THANKS A LOT... UMM...

ONE MORE TIME: RED!

I DIDN'T EXPECT TO SEE A POKÉMON THAT BIG... NOT HERE OF ALL PLACES!

WAS IT WILD OR WAS IT...

GYARADOS IS A WATER POKÉMON. AND IT'S NOT SUPPOSED TO LIVE IN PLACES LIKE THIS...

LIKE I FIGURED. SO... WHY?

THAT GYARADOS ISN'T WILD.

IT'S MY POKÉ-MON.

WHAAAAT?!!

I WAS RAISING IT...'TIL LAST WEEK, WHEN SOMEBODY STOLE IT.

WHEN IT CAME BACK... IT WASN'T THE NICE GYRADOS I KNEW...

I FOLLOWED IT...NOT HARD, SINCE IT WAS DESTROYING EVERYTHING IN ITS PATH...

.....

ANYWAY, THANKS PARTLY TO YOU, EVERYTHING'S OKAY N--

IT IS **NOT**!

IT'S NEVER *OKAY* WHEN A POKÉMON GOES BERSERK!

THOSE GUYS WHO STOLE GYARADOS MUSTA DONE IT!

I'M GOING TO GO KICK THEIR BUTTS!

WHERE DO YOU THINK YOU'RE GOING?

WHERE D'YOU THINK?! I'M... UH...

THOSE THIEVES... YOU SAID THEY WERE...

...WHERE?

LISTEN...

IF I KNEW, DON'T YOU THINK I'D *BE* THERE?!

HEY! MAYBE THE PROF KNOWS SOMETHING...

hmmm

?

POKÉMON CENTER.

PIK PIK PIK

PNG!

OHO, RED!

BEEN A WHILE!

AW, SHUCKS!

THAT'S PROFESSOR OAK. HE'S THE WORLD'S LEADING EXPERT ON POKÉMON.

THERE ARE KNOWN TO BE MORE THAN ONE HUNDRED VARIETIES OF POKÉMON...

...SCATTERED ALL OVER THE EARTH.

GETTING CLOSER TO COMPLETING YOUR POKÉDEX, RED?

'SMATTER OF FACT, I AM! I EVEN GOT SOME NEW DATA TODAY! TAKE A LOOK...

VWIP!

A HIGH-TECH EN-CYCLO-PEDIA.

A POKÉ-DEX?

GYARADOS

DATA

No. 130

Description
ATROCIOUS
Categories
Type 1/ Water
2/ Flying
Height 21' 04"
Weight 518.0 lb
Attacks
Dragon Rage
Bite
Hydro Pump

The evolved form of Magikarp. Rarely seen in the wild. Huge and vicious, it is capable of destroying entire cities in a rage. Can fire a Hyper-Beam from its mouth.

OHO-HO... GYARA-DOS...

BLAH BLAH BLAH!

YES, EV-OLVES FROM MAGI-KARP...

HYDRO PUMP...

WHENEVER I CATCH A POKEMON, ITS DATA AUTOMATIC-ALLY GETS INPUTTED.

TO INPUT ALL THE DATA...ON ALL THE POKÉMON...

THAT'S MY GOAL IN LIFE!

I'LL HAVE TO FIGHT WILD POKÉMON AND TOUGH TRAINERS ON THE WAY...

BUT I'LL BE A TOP POKÉMON TRAINER MYSELF ONE O' THESE...

OH YEAH! PROF! I NEED TO ASK YOU SOMETHING!

...THUS, CLEARLY...

KWIP!

YOU NEED TO ASK--?!

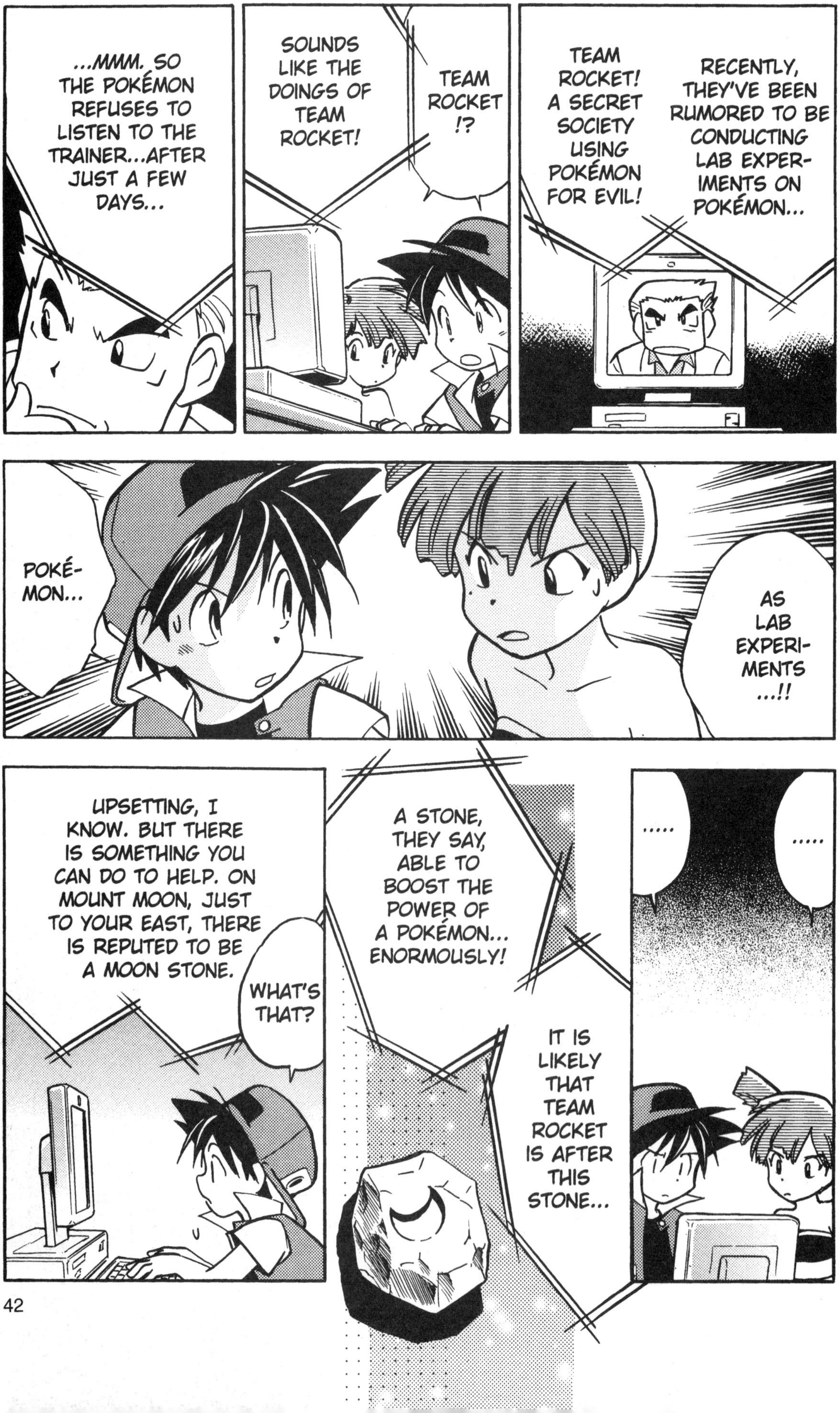
...MMM. SO THE POKÉMON REFUSES TO LISTEN TO THE TRAINER...AFTER JUST A FEW DAYS...
SOUNDS LIKE THE DOINGS OF TEAM ROCKET!
TEAM ROCKET !?
TEAM ROCKET! A SECRET SOCIETY USING POKÉMON FOR EVIL!
RECENTLY, THEY'VE BEEN RUMORED TO BE CONDUCTING LAB EXPER-IMENTS ON POKÉMON...
POKÉ-MON...
AS LAB EXPERI-MENTS ...!!
UPSETTING, I KNOW. BUT THERE IS SOMETHING YOU CAN DO TO HELP. ON MOUNT MOON, JUST TO YOUR EAST, THERE IS REPUTED TO BE A MOON STONE.
WHAT'S THAT?
A STONE, THEY SAY, ABLE TO BOOST THE POWER OF A POKÉMON... ENORMOUSLY!
.....
.....
IT IS LIKELY THAT TEAM ROCKET IS AFTER THIS STONE...

THAT DOES IT!

IF THE POKÉDEX GETS COMPLETED ...FINE!

BUT FIRST I'M GONNA SEARCH OUT THIS 'TEAM ROCKET" OR WHAT-EVER IT'S CALLED...

AND I'M GONNA KICK... THEIR ...

.....

WHAT IS IT?

I'M GOING WITH YOU!

HUH ?!

MOUNT MOON IS ON THE WAY TO MY HOME TOWN...

AND IF I GO WITH YOU, I'M BOUND TO RUN INTO A LOT OF TRAINERS I KNOW.

I MIGHT BE ABLE TO GET SOME INFORMATION ON THIS TEAM ROCKET TOO!

W-WAIT A MINUTE! Y-YOU DON'T THINK YOU CAN TAKE ON...

SSHHH

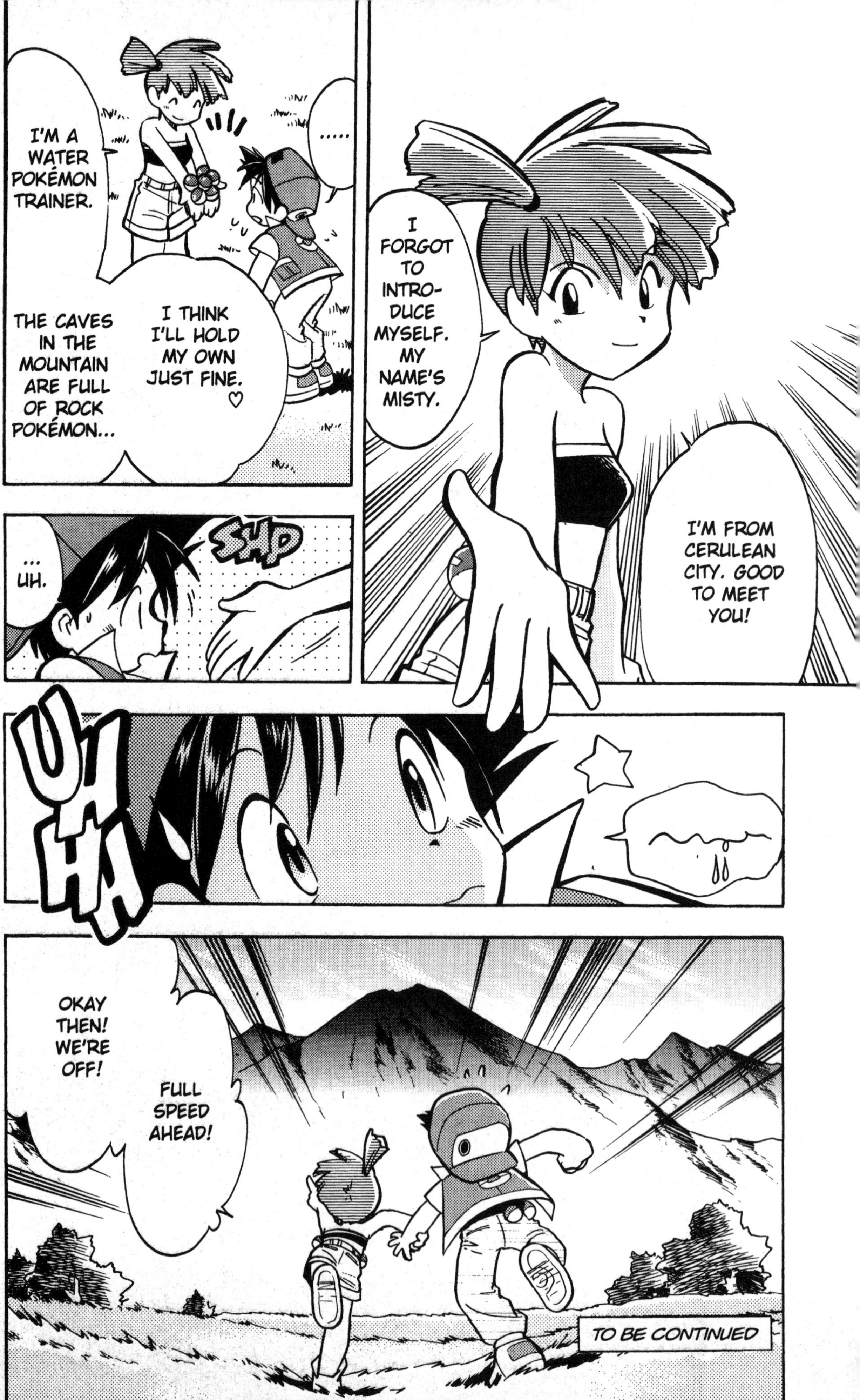

I'M A WATER POKÉMON TRAINER.
......
THE CAVES IN THE MOUNTAIN ARE FULL OF ROCK POKÉMON...
I THINK I'LL HOLD MY OWN JUST FINE. ♡
I FORGOT TO INTRO-DUCE MYSELF. MY NAME'S MISTY.
I'M FROM CERULEAN CITY. GOOD TO MEET YOU!
SHP
... UH.
UH HA
OKAY THEN! WE'RE OFF!
FULL SPEED AHEAD!
TO BE CONTINUED

IN THE NEXT ISSUE:

Misty and Red venture into the dark caves of Mount Moon!

Can little Pikachu defeat a raging Rhydon!?

Can Red defeat the Cerulean City Gym leader?

Bill and a Rattata get their bodies mixed up!

Can Red save the Rattata version of Bill from the frightening Fearow!?

Get the next exciting issue:
STARMIE SURPRISE!
on sale soon!

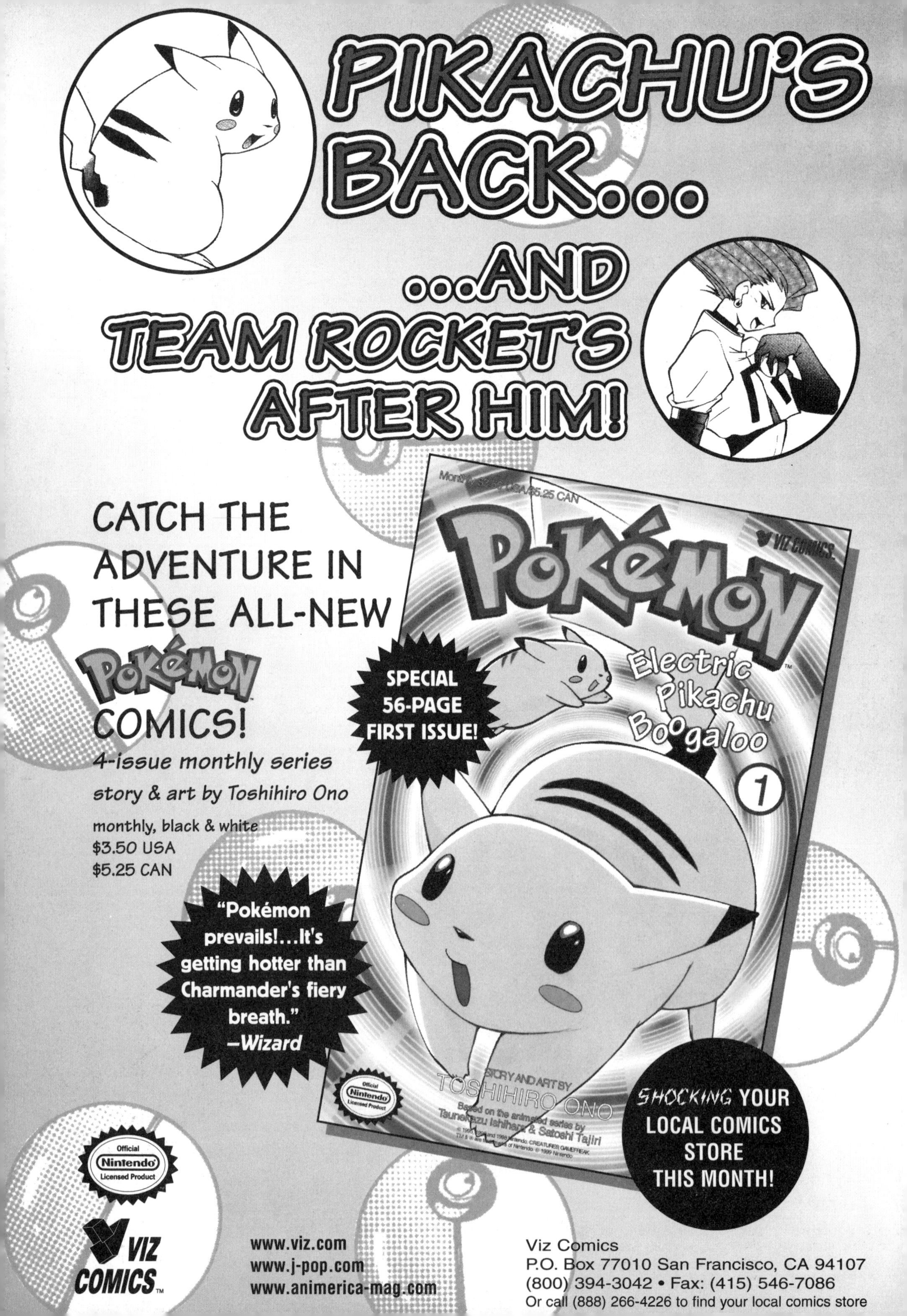

PIKACHU'S BACK...
...AND TEAM ROCKET'S AFTER HIM!
CATCH THE ADVENTURE IN THESE ALL-NEW
POKéMON
COMICS!
4-issue monthly series
story & art by Toshihiro Ono
monthly, black & white
$3.50 USA
$5.25 CAN
"Pokémon prevails!...It's getting hotter than Charmander's fiery breath." —Wizard
SPECIAL 56-PAGE FIRST ISSUE!
VIZ COMICS
POKéMON
Electric Pikachu Boogaloo
1
STORY AND ART BY TOSHIHIRO ONO
Based on the animated series by Tsunekazu Ishihara & Satoshi Tajiri
Official Nintendo Licensed Product
SHOCKING YOUR LOCAL COMICS STORE THIS MONTH!
Official Nintendo Licensed Product
VIZ COMICS
www.viz.com
www.j-pop.com
www.animerica-mag.com
Viz Comics
P.O. Box 77010 San Francisco, CA 94107
(800) 394-3042 • Fax: (415) 546-7086
Or call (888) 266-4226 to find your local comics store

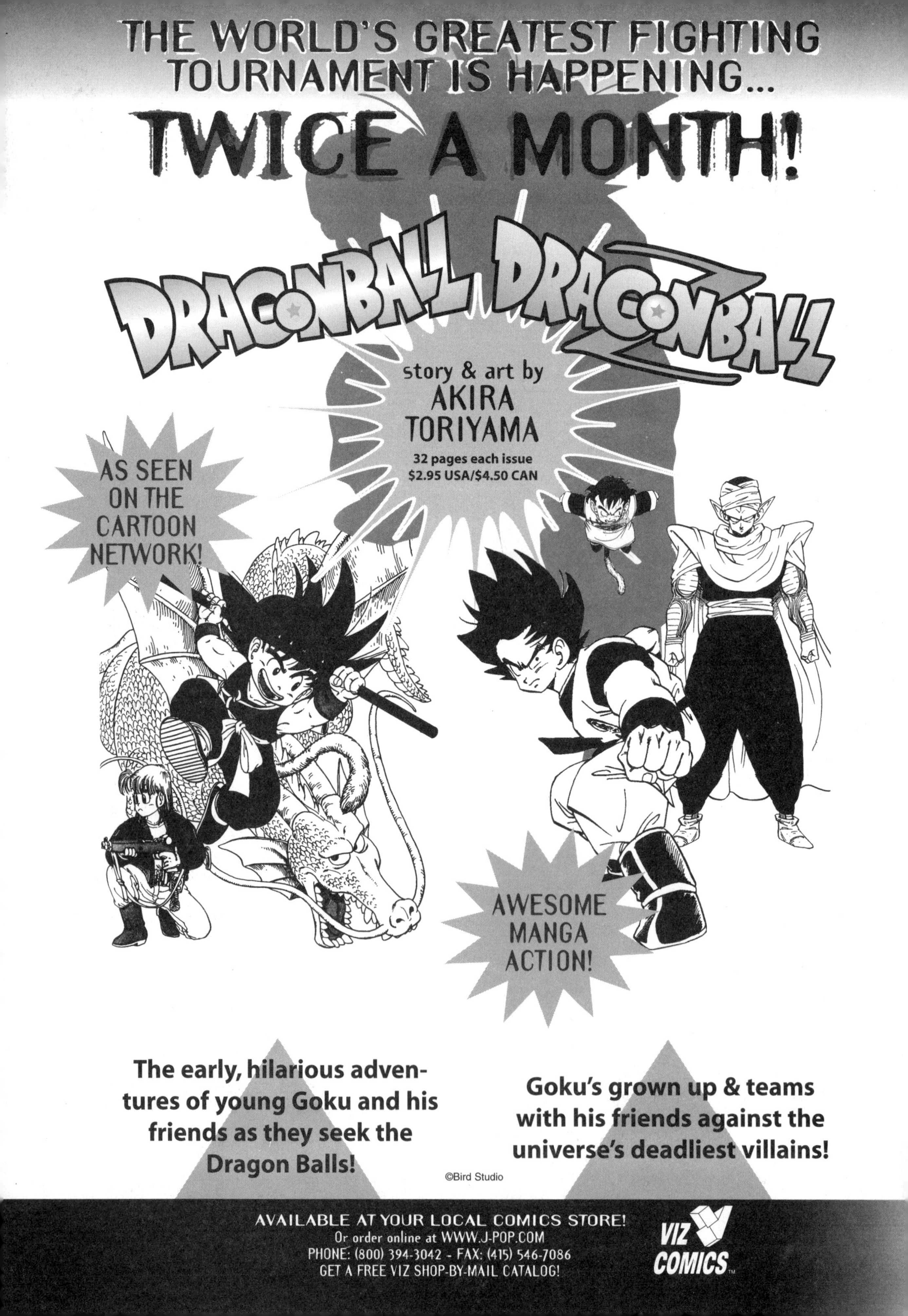

THE WORLD'S GREATEST FIGHTING TOURNAMENT IS HAPPENING...
TWICE A MONTH!
DRAGONBALL
DRAGONBALL Z
story & art by AKIRA TORIYAMA
32 pages each issue
$2.95 USA/$4.50 CAN
AS SEEN ON THE CARTOON NETWORK!
AWESOME MANGA ACTION!
The early, hilarious adventures of young Goku and his friends as they seek the Dragon Balls!
Goku's grown up & teams with his friends against the universe's deadliest villains!
©Bird Studio
AVAILABLE AT YOUR LOCAL COMICS STORE!
Or order online at WWW.J-POP.COM
PHONE: (800) 394-3042 - FAX: (415) 546-7086
GET A FREE VIZ SHOP-BY-MAIL CATALOG!
VIZ COMICS™